This book belongs to

....

and I wish for

....

....

Hi! We're the Wish sisters!

I'm Flick and this is my little sister, Birdie.

We're not the Wish sisters because it's our last name, but because there's so much wishing in our house.

'Gah!'

It all started when our Granny Aggie found an imp in an old bottle and wished for us to have unlimited wishes!

You'd think having unlimited wishes would be fun. And it is! It's also a whole lot of trouble.

'My name is Imp,
not he or she,
just a plain old imp
I be.'

The imp likes to twist wishes and make them go wrong. It twisted Granny Aggie's wish so that only Birdie can wish.

Now I really have to be the best big sister ever to help keep Birdie's wishes under control!

The Wish Sisters

The Christmas Wish

Allison Rushby

illustrated by Karen Blair

UQP

1

A very squelchy Christmas

Flick was quiet as she followed her family back inside their house. She and her little sister, Birdie, had just finished helping put up their outdoor Christmas lights. Flick usually loved getting ready for Christmas. But she wasn't interested in decorating this year. This was because she was feeling a bit glum. It would be her family's first

Christmas without their Granny Aggie. Granny Aggie had adored Christmas and Flick had been her special helper. 'Just like my own little elf!' Granny Aggie had always said.

'Why don't you two go and play with Santa's workshop?' Flick's dad suggested.

This was a fun wooden toy Birdie had been given last Christmas and she was finally big enough to enjoy it. It had nine little doors and a little wooden elf lived inside each one. Each elf looked different. They wore different coloured felt hats and carried different coloured presents.

Flick took Birdie into the living room and put her down on the rug. Then Flick fetched the Santa's workshop toy. She sat next to her little sister and started playing.

'Bleh,' Birdie said after a while.

Flick sighed. She knew what Birdie meant. She also felt a bit 'bleh'. She didn't want to think about Christmas.

Flick glanced over at her very favourite photo, sitting on top of the dresser. It was of her, Birdie and Granny Aggie. Flick was holding a tiny new baby Birdie, and Granny Aggie was holding up a t-shirt she'd just given Flick. It said, *Best Big Sister Ever.* They both had huge smiles on their faces. Flick loved that t-shirt and ever since that day, she had decided to try to truly be the best big sister ever.

Flick knew that Granny Aggie wouldn't want them to be sad at Christmas. But Flick didn't know how to have a fun Christmas without Granny Aggie.

Flick's mum passed by with a basket of washing. 'Oh, dear,' she said, spotting Flick's face. She put the basket on the table. 'Maybe we should do something nice today.' She thought for a moment. 'I know. How about we make gingerbread houses again? We loved making those last year.'

Flick's dad appeared in the doorway with another basket of washing. 'That's a great idea!' he said. 'If you start making the gingerbread, I'll pop to the shops and pick up icing sugar and gumdrops and things.'

'Gah!' Birdie clapped her hands. She seemed to like the sound of gingerbread houses.

'What do you think, Flick?' her mum asked.

Flick looked at Birdie. She wanted to be the best big sister ever and show Birdie how fun Christmas could be, just like Granny Aggie would have. 'I guess so,' she finally replied.

'I'll check what else we might need.' Flick's dad disappeared into the kitchen. 'Uh oh,' he called out. 'We don't have any ground ginger. That will hold us up a bit, I'm afraid. You can't make gingerbread without ginger.'

'Bleh!' Birdie shook her head. **'Bleh, bleh, bleh.'** It looked like Birdie didn't want to wait. She wanted to make gingerbread houses NOW.

'Oli might have some ginger,' Flick suggested. Oli was her best friend. He lived right next door. 'I can go and …' Flick trailed off. She wrinkled her nose. Something smelled funny. She picked up one foot. Then the other. There was something soft and squishy between her toes. She looked down.

There was dirt under her feet! In fact, the whole floor was now dark, squelchy dirt. Flick gasped as green shoots began to pop out of the ground. They came right up to her head! She bent down quickly and picked up Birdie.

'Gah!' Birdie said, staring around at the field of green leaves.

'Wow,' a voice came from the back door. Flick couldn't see him, but she recognised Oli's voice. 'I know you talked about getting some indoor plants, but this is something else!'

2

Gumdrops and yoo-hoos

Flick's mum and dad used their arms to slash through the plants. Oli did the same.

Finally, everyone was standing in the centre of the living room with Flick and Birdie.

'What's going on?' Flick asked.

Flick's mum reached down and yanked out one of the green stems. There was something large and knobbly on the end. She dusted off some chunks of dirt. 'This is ginger.'

'Ah,' Flick said. That explained a lot. She turned to Oli. 'We want to make gingerbread, but we don't have any ground ginger.'

'My mum might have some,' Oli said. 'I'll go and check.' He took off, slashing his way back through the plants like an explorer in the jungle.

Flick knew that Oli wouldn't think it was strange that their living room had become a field of ginger plants. This was because he knew all about the wishes.

Flick's Granny Aggie had left Flick and

Birdie an imp in a special old bottle. The imp could grant unlimited wishes! But the imp had twisted Granny Aggie's wish. It said Granny Aggie had given her wishes to her grand*babies* not grand*children*, and because Flick wasn't a baby, she couldn't wish!

The imp loved to twist wishes. Whatever Birdie wished for, the imp would try to twist it. There had been a lot of wishing going on at Flick's house lately. There had been visits from unicorns, giant-sized babies, rainbow-coloured cats and, now, ginger fields in the living room.

'This isn't the kind of ginger we need, Birdie,' Flick's dad said. 'We need ground ginger. It comes in a little glass bottle.'

'Gah, gah, gah,' Birdie said. The field of ginger disappeared.

'I came in a little glass bottle too,' a voice said.

Flick's family all turned to see a creature with curly purple hair, little stubby horns, hooves and a cheeky gap-toothed grin standing on top of Birdie's Santa's workshop toy. It was the imp!

Flick should have known the imp would turn up if they were making gingerbread houses. The imp *loved* to eat. Almost as much as it loved twisting wishes.

'I've got the ginger!' Oli ran in through the back door, holding a little glass jar.

'Thanks, Oli,' Flick's dad said. 'I'll put two jars on the shopping list. One for us and one for your mum.'

'I don't know much about this Christmas business,' the imp said. 'But I do know you'd better get a lot of those gumdrops you were talking about. Because I think I'm going to like those!'

While Flick's dad went to the shops, Flick, Oli, Birdie and the imp found Granny Aggie's gingerbread recipe. With the help of Flick's mum, they used Granny Aggie's cherry-red mixer to make the dough. Then they rolled the gingerbread flat and used special cookie cutters to cut out the walls and roofs of the little houses.

'That's a lot of gingerbread houses,' Flick said, looking at the baking sheets. 'And we've still got some dough left over. Could we make some gingerbread people as well?'

'I suppose someone has to live in all those houses!' Flick's mum chuckled. She found the gingerbread person cookie cutter and everyone took a turn at stamping.

As Flick watched Birdie stamp, she remembered the stamping she'd done with Granny Aggie. And that made her smile.

Soon the gingerbread was in the oven. It smelled delicious. Sweet and warm and gingery.

Flour

Just as it was coming out of the oven, Flick's dad arrived back from the shops. He had icing sugar and gumdrops and musk sticks and all sorts of lollies to decorate the houses with.

'Gah!' Birdie looked like she wanted to start decorating right away.

'We have to wait for the gingerbread to cool first,' Flick told her little sister. 'Let's go out in the backyard and play while we wait,' she added quickly. She didn't want Birdie making any wishes to cool the gingerbread down fast. The imp might turn the kitchen into an ice-skating rink. Or the North Pole. Complete with polar bears!

'I'll stay here and protect the gingerbread,' the imp said.

'Hmmm . . .' Flick's dad replied. 'I might stay here and watch you protecting the gingerbread. Just in case.'

Flick, Oli and Birdie had just walked outside when they heard a familiar voice.

'Yoo-hoo! Oh, yoo-hoo!'

3

Mrs Mortlake's house

'Hello, Mrs Mortlake.' Flick waved. She gave Birdie, who was perched on her hip, a warning look. She didn't want to hear any rude 'blehs' from her little sister.

Mrs Mortlake was their other next-door neighbour. She wasn't a bad person. She was just a bit nosy. She even had a special stool beside her fence so she could see into her neighbours' yards. And this was exactly what she was doing now – standing on the stool and peering into Flick's garden.

'Are you cooking?' Mrs Mortlake asked. 'Something smells wonderful!'

Flick nodded. 'We're baking gingerbread.'

Flick's mum came out into the backyard. 'Hello, Mrs Mortlake,' she said.

'I was just saying to the children that the gingerbread smells lovely. So Christmassy,' Mrs Mortlake said. 'I'm afraid I haven't even put up my Christmas tree. It doesn't seem worth the trouble. My daughter and her family live in Scotland now, so it would only be for me. I wish

I could spend Christmas with them, but it's just too expensive.'

Flick felt sorry for Mrs Mortlake. She knew how it felt to miss your family at Christmas. 'We can help you put up your tree,' Flick offered. 'Can't we, Oli?'

'Sure,' Oli said. 'I put ours up. And decorated it. But I only put decorations on the top half because Max takes them off. It looks a bit funny.'

Max was Oli's little brother. He was the same age as Birdie.

'We'll pop over in a bit, Mrs Mortlake,' Flick's mum said.

'Oh. Well, that would be lovely.' Mrs Mortlake seemed touched by their offer. 'Thank you all very much. I'll go and find the tree now.' She disappeared behind the fence.

Flick's mum, Flick and Oli looked at one another.

'What could go wrong?' Oli said.

Birdie clapped her hands and laughed.

Flick gave her sister yet another stern look. 'No wishing, Birdie,' she said.

Flick's family really didn't want Mrs Mortlake to find out about the wishes. The imp had warned them to keep the wishes to themselves and Mrs Mortlake wasn't very good at keeping secrets.

Also, her niece was a television news reporter. If Mrs Mortlake found out about the wishes, the whole world would soon know!

'Do be careful, dear,' Mrs Mortlake said as she took yet another decoration off Birdie. 'Some of my ornaments are quite delicate. Especially the angel that goes on top.'

Flick passed Birdie a candy cane made from felt. Birdie couldn't break that. 'You can put this one on the tree,' Flick said.

'Oh, that's quite special too. From a trip to Germany, you know.'

'Bleh,' Birdie said grumpily. **'Bleh, bleh, bleh.'**

'Birdie,' Flick's mum warned.

Flick helped her little sister carefully put the candy cane on the tree.

'Oopsie!' Mrs Mortlake stepped in as Birdie reached for a pretty ornament of Santa's sleigh, stacked full of shiny presents. 'Why don't you take this one instead.' She handed Birdie a plain wooden star.

Birdie looked at the star. Then she looked at Flick and pointed towards home. Birdie clearly wanted to go and decorate the gingerbread houses.

'Come on, Birdie,' Flick said. 'The tree will look really pretty when it's done.'

Birdie muttered something under her breath. Then she blew a big raspberry.

At the same time, Flick thought she heard a noise.

'Did you hear that?' Oli asked. 'It sounded like …'

Flick nodded. 'I know. It sounded like a snorty laugh.'

4

Some interesting ornaments

Flick and Oli looked around themselves. They had definitely heard the imp's snorty laugh. But they couldn't see it anywhere.

'How about this one next?' Mrs Mortlake passed Flick a silver snowflake. She paused, squinting as she looked at the tree. 'That's funny, I don't remember owning so many purple ornaments.'

Flick turned her attention back to the tree.

'Oh, no ...' Oli said.

Flick's mum suddenly began to cough. Loudly.

'Oh, dear. That doesn't sound good. I'll fetch you a glass of water.' Mrs Mortlake rushed off towards the kitchen.

Flick's mum followed her, giving the children a look as she went.

Flick nodded. She could see the problem. The tree was now covered in purple ornaments. And not just any purple ornaments. Every single one was a miniature imp!

Flick leaned in to peer closely at them. Each imp was different. There was an ice-skating imp, a surfing imp, an imp sticking its tongue out, an imp doing disco moves and even an imp eating a big bowl of ice cream!

'The ice cream one is my favourite,' a voice came from above.

Flick looked up. The imp was perched right at the top of the tree where Mrs Mortlake's special angel was supposed to go.

But the imp was no angel.

Birdie clapped her hands and laughed. She liked the imp's Christmas tree.

'I'm guessing Birdie wished for the tree to be finished,' Flick said.

'And this is your twist.'

'I do love to twist.' The imp did a funny twisting dance. The tree swayed as the imp moved about.

Flick and Oli looked at one another in horror. There wasn't a moment to lose. They both began urgently plucking the ornaments from the tree. But there were so many!

Flick plucked faster and faster. She wanted to get the imp ornaments off and Mrs Mortlake's special ornaments on before she came back. Even if Mrs Mortlake was a bit fussy, Flick wanted her to have a nice Christmas. She'd looked so sad about not spending it with her family.

It didn't take long for Flick to come up with an idea.

'You know,' she said to the imp, 'if Mrs Mortlake sees these ornaments, there'll be a big fuss. And if there's a big fuss, we'll never get to decorate the gingerbread houses. And, more importantly, *eat* the gingerbread houses.'

'Ooohhh …' the imp replied from its perch. It paused. 'So what you're saying is, if the tree is decorated properly, we'll be able to go home and eat the gingerbread.'

'Decorate the gingerbread houses, yes,' Flick said.

'And eat them.'

'*After* we've decorated them.'

The imp thought for a moment. 'Hmmm ... maybe you should make your wish again, Birdie.'

'Gah, gah, gah,' Birdie said.

There was a bright flash of colour.

Just like that, the tree was perfectly decorated with Mrs Mortlake's own ornaments.

'I personally think mine looked way better,' the imp said.

Flick held up the angel. 'Hurry!' she said.

'You're just no fun!' The imp stomped a foot and the Christmas tree shook. But then Flick blinked and the imp was gone and the angel was on top of the tree.

Just in time.

The doorbell rang and Mrs Mortlake hurried past them to open it. Flick's mum followed behind her. She looked relieved to see the imp ornaments were gone.

It was Flick's dad at the door.

'I just wanted to see how you're getting on,' he said as Mrs Mortlake brought him into the living room. 'We've got so much gingerbread. I thought you might like to come and decorate a gingerbread house with us, Mrs Mortlake. Your mum and Max are going to join us too, Oli. I thought we could set up a table in the backyard. We'll decorate the houses and make afternoon tea of it. We could invite Mr Tran too.'

'Why, that sounds delightful, thank you. I'll bring a big jug of iced tea.' Mrs Mortlake looked pleased. She turned to view the tree. 'Oh! Just look at that! What a wonderful job you've done.' A tear came to her eye. 'Thank you,' she said.

Flick was glad to see Mrs Mortlake didn't look glum anymore. And Flick felt a little better too. Decorating Mrs Mortlake's tree had made her remember happy times decorating the family tree with Granny Aggie. Maybe Christmas was catching on Honeysuckle Street? 'Come on,' Flick said to Oli and Birdie. 'Let's go and see if Mr Tran can come for afternoon tea too.'

5

A very impish problem

'Well, hello there,' Mr Tran said when he opened his front door. 'What a pleasant surprise.'

'Hello, Mr Tran,' Flick said.

'Wait, where's Beans?' Oli asked. Beans was Mr Tran's sausage dog and Oli often took him for walks. Oli *loved* dogs.

'Yes, where *is* Beans?' Flick was

surprised too. Beans always greeted them at the door.

'Oh.' Mr Tran's face fell. 'I'm afraid Beans has been a bit unwell. He ate something in the garden and it made him sick. He had to stay at the vet overnight.'

'Oh, no!' Flick and Oli said together.

'He's all right. He just needed some medicine. I can pick him up this afternoon. I must admit, the house feels very quiet without him.'

Flick could see that Mr Tran needed cheering up as well. She told him about the gingerbread house decorating and invited him to come along. Hopefully it would take his mind off poor Beans.

Mr Tran's face lit up. 'I'd love to come. What a wonderful way to honour your Granny Aggie. I remember last year when you made those gingerbread houses with her. You all had so much fun. You must be missing her very much.'

Flick nodded. They were. But she loved it when people talked about Granny Aggie. 'You must miss her too,' Flick said. Mr Tran had been good friends with Granny Aggie.

Flick felt a bit bad that she hadn't thought about this before. She'd been too caught up in feeling glum. But then she began to realise something. Christmas hadn't been special just because Granny

Aggie was with them. Christmas had been special because Granny Aggie *made* it special. Because she got everyone to come together and have fun.

They arranged for Mr Tran to come over in about an hour so they'd have time to set everything up.

Back at the house, the imp had, thankfully, not eaten the gingerbread. Flick's parents sat Birdie in her highchair so she could see what was going on. Then they got busy putting all the lollies into bowls and making the icing.

'Oh, I almost forgot,' Flick's dad said.

'I bought a few other things at the shops.' He grabbed some items from the bench. 'Like them?' He put on a pair of glasses that looked like plum puddings. He also had a pair that looked like Christmas trees. 'And I bought this for Mrs Mortlake.' He held up a fancy tin. There was a picture on the lid of a cottage in the snow.

'What's inside?' Flick asked.

'Shortbread biscuits. They're running a special competition where you can win a trip to Scotland. Mrs Mortlake's always talking about not being able to visit her daughter. I know she wants to go. So I put her name down.'

'That was nice of you,' Flick's mum said. 'When are they drawing the winner?'

'This afternoon, apparently.'

'How exciting,' Flick's mum replied.

'I know I'm excited!' a voice piped up. 'For gumdrops. And musk sticks. And icing. And gingerbread!'

Everyone turned. The imp was sitting on one of the kitchen stools, waving its hands in the air.

Flick gasped, realising they had a problem. A big problem! Oli's mum, baby Max, Mrs Mortlake and Mr Tran were all coming over. How was the imp going to decorate gingerbread houses with them all without being noticed?

Flick knew she was going to have to find a clever way to include the imp in the afternoon's fun.

But how?

6

An adorable elf

'You've got a funny look on your face,' the imp said to Flick.

'I do?' Flick said, thinking fast. There was no way the imp could miss out on decorating the gingerbread houses. It was so excited. And Flick wanted the imp's Christmas to be special too.

Flick spied the Christmas tree glasses on

the bench. And suddenly she knew what to do. She leaned over to Oli and whispered to him. Oli's eyes widened. Then he nodded.

'I'll be right back,' he said. And then he shot out the back door.

'Gah?' Birdie said from her highchair.

'My thoughts exactly,' the imp said. 'What's going on?'

'Well.' Flick picked up the Christmas tree glasses. 'We've got a little problem. The neighbours are coming to decorate the gingerbread houses. But you can't be seen. How can you decorate a house with us if no one's allowed to see you?'

'We could uninvite the neighbours,' the imp said helpfully.

'Or you could wear a costume!' Flick said.

Oli came bursting back through the door, panting. 'I got it!' He held something up. Something small and cute and green.

Oli had returned with a costume he had bought for his dog, Rosie. It was a cute green elf suit. It had fake arms at the front that held a present and there was even a pointy hat with a bell on the end.

The imp was not happy about having to get dressed up. But Flick had a plan. She let the imp have a gumdrop for putting one arm into the costume. Then she gave it half a musk stick for putting the other arm in. And finally, Flick let the imp have the rest of the musk stick for putting the hat on.

'One last thing,' Flick said. She grabbed the Christmas tree glasses off the bench and put them on the imp. It was a pretty good disguise. Almost all of the imp's curly purple fur was hidden.

It looked adorable.

'You look very … festive,' Flick's dad said, fighting a laugh.

'I want another gumdrop. Please,' the imp said sulkily.

Flick gave the imp another gumdrop.

'Green is definitely your colour,' Flick's mum added.

'Purple's my colour,' the imp grumbled.

'We'll get one of Rosie's beds and put it under the table for you,' Flick said. 'Then if anyone sees you they'll think it's Rosie sleeping. The bed will be comfy to sit on and you can build your gingerbread house down there. That way you can still join in.'

'I don't care where I sit. As long as there's gingerbread, it's the perfect spot for me,' the imp said, sounding a bit happier.

Flick's family and Oli set up two folding tables outside and covered them with

Christmas tablecloths printed with tiny presents. Flick's dad had bought some paper plates in the shape of reindeers, along with reindeer napkins and matching paper cups.

Flick's dad set out the pieces for a gingerbread house on each person's plate. There were walls and a roof and even a tiny chimney. Then he put out the bowls of lollies and filled piping bags with icing.

Flick and Oli found some tinsel and wrapped it around the chairs. Everything looked very Christmassy.

Lastly, they placed Rosie's bed and a blanket under the table and set up the imp's decorating station. Now the imp had a secret spot to decorate its own gingerbread house.

'Yoo-hoo! Oh, yoo-hoo!' a voice called out. Mrs Mortlake had arrived.

Flick turned to Oli, suddenly remembering his comment from earlier. 'What could go wrong?' he'd said.

Flick gulped. She could think of so many things that could go wrong. Birdie might wish for a real Christmas tree and a forest might appear in the back garden. She might wish for Santa to appear and her family would be whisked away to the North Pole. Maybe she'd like the gingerbread so much she'd turn their house into an actual gingerbread house!

But then Flick remembered something else. That first time she had made gingerbread houses, everything *had* gone wrong. It had been a very hot day and the icing wouldn't stick. The houses wouldn't stay up and the lollies had slid off.

Flick had been disappointed, but Granny Aggie had just laughed. 'It doesn't matter,' she'd said. 'What matters is we're having fun together.'

Flick realised it was the same with the wishes. They might go wrong. But if they did, everyone would come together to fix them.

Somehow, it would be all right.

7

Christmas wishes

Oli's mum, Claire, arrived with baby Max. Not long after, Mr Tran turned up and completed the party. Mrs Mortlake poured everyone a lovely cup of iced tea and they all got started.

Decorating the gingerbread houses was lots of fun. Just like last time, the day was warm and the icing went a bit runny, but it didn't matter. Somehow everyone got the lollies to stick onto their houses. And while some of the houses were a bit wonky, when they broke one up to share, it tasted great.

'Your Granny Aggie always did have the best gingerbread recipe,' Mrs Mortlake told Flick. 'She had a special touch with baking.'

Flick's family nodded. She really had.

'Oh!' Claire said, then laughed. 'I just felt something furry under the table. I completely forgot Rosie was under there napping. She's been so quiet.'

'Er, yes,' Flick's mum said. 'Now, everyone, don't forget about the gingerbread people. They need decorating

too.' She quickly changed the topic.

Flick's mum passed the gingerbread people around and everyone started decorating them. They looked so sweet with their gumdrop eyes and icing smiles.

Until Mr Tran started being silly. He gave one of his gingerbread people a big, toothy grin. He gave another sticky-up hair. Then he made an angry-looking little gingerbread person with fangs. He pretended it was chomping lollies off the table. Everyone laughed. Mr Tran was so funny.

'Oh! I've just remembered something.' Flick's dad jumped up and ran inside the house. He came back with the tin of shortbread. He gave it to Mrs Mortlake and told her all about the competition.

'How kind of you to think of me,' Mrs Mortlake said, a tear in her eye again. 'I would love to be with my daughter and her family for Christmas. But I'm afraid I've never won anything. Not even a raffle. I wish I was that sort of person …'

'Did someone say wishes?' a voice came from under the table. 'Christmas wishes?'

'What was that, dear?' Mrs Mortlake turned to Flick.

'Er, nothing, Mrs Mortlake,' Flick said quickly. 'I was just thinking about … Christmas. And, um … wishes.' She picked a piece of gingerbread off her plate and waved it underneath the table. It disappeared in seconds. Hopefully that would keep the imp busy for a bit longer.

'Wouldn't it be lovely to be granted a Christmas wish!' Mrs Mortlake continued.

Everyone in Flick's family, plus Oli, shook their heads. Hard.

'Wishes can go wrong, Mrs Mortlake,' Flick warned.

'Really, really wrong,' Oli agreed.

'Gah!' Birdie said.

'Surely wishes wouldn't go wrong at Christmas!' Mrs Mortlake argued.

'I'm pretty sure they would,' Flick replied.

'You all seem to know a lot about

wishes,' Mr Tran chimed in, a twinkle in his eye.

Flick had wondered before how much Granny Aggie had told Mr Tran.

'Well, I think a Christmas wish would be wonderful.' Mrs Mortlake simply could not stop talking about wishes. 'Let's make a game of it. Come on, everyone. Let's go around the table and see what everyone would wish for.'

8

When wishes come true

Mr Tran glanced at his watch. 'Maybe I should go first? I'll have to pick up Beans soon. Now, let me see. A Christmas wish …' His gaze moved around the table. 'I know! I wish for Mrs Mortlake to win that trip to Scotland.'

'Bleh.' It didn't sound like Birdie agreed. Flick guessed her little sister was still cranky about Mrs Mortlake's ornaments. Still, at least Birdie hadn't …

'Gah, gah, gah,' Birdie added after a pause.

Flick's family and Oli all froze in their seats. Was that a wish?

A muffled ringing noise started up. Everyone looked around. Someone's phone was ringing.

'Oh, goodness! That's *my* phone.' Mrs Mortlake grabbed her handbag. 'What's it doing ringing? I don't get that many calls.' She finally dug it out and answered it.

'Hello? Yes, this is she.'

Mrs Mortlake's mouth dropped open. 'I have? Really?'

Her eyes lit up. 'Well, yes. Thank you very much.'

Mrs Mortlake hung up. She sat for a moment, fanning her face. 'I don't believe it. I won that trip to Scotland! I leave tomorrow!' She was grinning from ear to ear.

'Goodness!' Mr Tran said. 'That wish came true very easily.' He glanced at Flick and Birdie and smiled.

'How wonderful!' Claire chimed in.

Flick's family and Oli all looked at each other before congratulating Mrs Mortlake as well. Flick was very happy for Mrs Mortlake. But she was also a bit worried. She stuck her head under the table.

The imp looked up. 'Hi there, Flick. Got any more musk sticks?'

'No. Not unless you tell me what the twist is on that wish. You're not sending Mrs Mortlake to some place called Scotland in America or something, are you?'

The imp cackled. 'I didn't think of that! The thing is, I don't want to twist this wish. If Mrs Mortlake is away, Birdie will be able to make lots and lots of fun wishes without anyone peering over the fence!'

Flick thought about this. It actually made a lot of sense. She picked a musk stick off her gingerbread house. Then she passed it to the imp under the table. The imp deserved it.

Flick had never seen Mrs Mortlake so excited. 'I can't believe I'll be with my family for Christmas! Thank you so much for entering the competition for me!' Mrs Mortlake clapped her hands together. 'Now, I really do think everyone else should take their turn at wishing. Mr Tran's wish came true. Maybe everyone else's will too?'

Flick gulped.

'Well, I don't mind having a go,' Claire spoke up.

'Mum,' Oli said quickly. 'I don't think …'

'Oh, come on, Oli,' Claire said. 'Wishing's fun! I was just thinking, I've always wanted to have a white Christmas. The three of us have never even seen snow. It would be so magical. So that would be my wish. For a white Christmas.'

Birdie was looking at the sky, her hands in the air.

'Birdie!' Flick warned.

But it was too late.

'Gah!' Birdie said. **'Gah, gah, gah!'**

9

Ding, ding, ding

Flick expected snow to begin falling from the sky. Instead, everyone's phones began to ding.

'A weather alert!' Mrs Mortlake said after checking her phone. 'It says we're about to have a freak cold snap. Oh, I hope that doesn't mean hail. I've just done some planting in my garden!'

Mr Tran jumped up from the table. 'I'd best go and collect Beans from the vet now if there's going to be a storm. Thank you for a lovely afternoon. It cheered me up so much. Christmas is looking much brighter.'

When Mr Tran was gone, Flick ducked her head under the table once more. 'Imp,' she said, 'what's the twist? It's not going to hail, is it? That would hurt!'

The imp was still snacking on gingerbread. Sometimes Flick thought it had more than one stomach. Maybe it did? 'Hailing gumdrops would be fun!' it said. 'But once again, I didn't do anything. Why would I? This is my first Christmas.

I want to see snow too!'

Sounds of amazement came from above the table. Flick stopped quizzing the imp and sat up.

And that's when she saw the first snowflakes falling from the sky.

Flick forgot about the imp then. And she forgot about worrying about the wishes.

Flick stood and stared with everyone else as the snowflakes floated through the air, carried on the breeze. She caught one of the snowflakes in her hand and watched it melt away.

It *was* magical.

Flick picked Birdie up out of her highchair. They reached up together, catching snowflake after snowflake.

'I can't believe it. It really is a white Christmas!' Claire said.

All the adults agreed – they'd never seen anything like it.

Thanks to the imp's magic, the snow soon built up into soft mounds.

Flick scooped up the imp from under the table. And before it could complain, she wrapped Rosie's blanket tight around it.

'Oh, look at Rosie, snug as a bug!' Mrs Mortlake said.

Flick and Oli took Birdie, Max and

'Rosie' over near the swing set so the imp wouldn't be spotted by the adults. Then they began to play. They ran about throwing snowballs – *thwack, thwack!* They made snow angels – *swoosh, swoosh!* And they tried to catch snowflakes on their tongues.

The imp wasn't very impressed with the snowflakes. 'I thought they'd be sugary sweet,' it said.

Still, they all agreed that snow was lots of fun.

The problem was, it was also cold.

Flick's parents ran inside and grabbed as many coats and jackets as they could find. Everyone wrapped up just like 'Rosie'.

'Come on, let's make a snowman!' Flick suggested.

Together they began to build a small snowman. They gave it gumdrops for eyes. They broke off some musk stick to make a little nose. And they found a banana lolly to make a smile.

Birdie and Max loved the snowman. They clapped and laughed.

But as the snow continued to fall, it got colder and colder.

Max began to squirm. Oli took his little brother over to his mum. Flick took Birdie too.

'I might take Max home and find his little winter suit,' Claire said.

Birdie watched Claire and Max start towards their house. Birdie cried out. It looked like she didn't want her friend to leave.

'It's okay, Birdie,' Flick said. 'Max will be back soon.'

Birdie's bottom lip trembled.

'Uh oh,' Oli said. 'We need a distraction.' He picked two gingerbread people off a plate on the table. Then he turned to Birdie. 'Look!'

Oli made the gingerbread people dance. He made them leapfrog. And he made them stand on each other's heads.

Birdie began to laugh. She giggled. She chortled. She cackled. The gingerbread people were the funniest thing she had ever seen!

And then …

'Gah!' Birdie said. **'Gah, gah, gah!'**

10

When gingerbread goes bad

'Oh, no,' Flick groaned. She couldn't imagine what Birdie might have wished for now.

For a moment, all was still. And then Oli jumped.

'Yikes!' He dropped the gingerbread people onto the table. 'The gingerbread people are *moving*,' he said. 'They're

moving by themselves! Flick, look!' Oli pointed at the plate.

Flick stared in horror as the gingerbread people began to stir. One by one they stretched. They stood. And then … they were off, leaving tiny footprints in the snow.

At first the adults didn't notice.

But then one of the gingerbread people streaked across the table, straight past Mrs Mortlake.

'What was that?' Mrs Mortlake said, alarmed. 'Was that a rat?'

The gingerbread person seemed to take offence to that. It ran back across the table and climbed on top of Mrs

Mortlake's decorated gingerbread house. Then it shook its fist at Mrs Mortlake. It was no rat!

Mrs Mortlake jumped up. 'Oh my goodness!' she said. 'They're … alive!' She reached out a finger and poked the little gingerbread person.

Unfortunately for Mrs Mortlake, it was the one with fangs. It leaned over and bit Mrs Mortlake's finger. 'Oh! Oh, I …' Mrs Mortlake staggered. She swooned.

Thankfully, Flick's dad saw Mrs Mortlake swaying. He ran around and caught her just in time. Then he helped her back into her chair.

Meanwhile, the other

gingerbread people were darting here and there. They were getting up to all kinds of mischief.

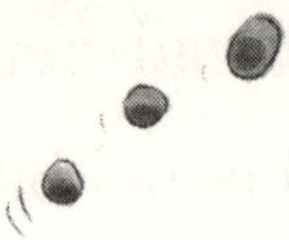

One gingerbread person stood in a lolly bowl and began to throw gumdrops at everyone. Another jumped on Flick's mum's shoulder and batted at her earrings. A third one jumped into the jug of iced tea and went for a swim.

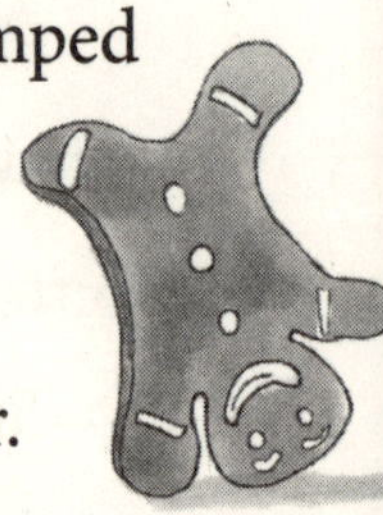

They couldn't have been naughtier.

Mrs Mortlake moaned in her chair.

'Birdie!' Flick's mum came over. She took Birdie from Flick and popped her into her highchair. 'It is not

acceptable to have the baked goods bite our guests.'

'Bleh,' Birdie said. It seemed like she didn't entirely agree.

But then the gingerbread person with fangs – the one who had bitten Mrs Mortlake – jumped up onto Birdie's highchair tray.

Birdie startled. She looked scared. Flick guessed she was worried about being bitten.

'Gah!' Birdie said quickly. **'Gah, gah, gah!'**

All of the gingerbread people immediately fell down in their places, and the table got busy tidying itself up. Lollies marched back into bowls. The tablecloth straightened itself. And splashes of iced tea slurped back into the jug.

'Gah!' Birdie said.

'What's that, Birdie?' Flick asked nervously.

But Birdie wasn't talking to Flick. She was talking to the imp.

'Don't mind if I do!' The imp crawled out from under the table, reached up and took the fanged gingerbread person from Birdie's highchair tray. And then it chomped its head off.

'*Yummy!*'

11

Mrs Mortlake's win

The snow had stopped falling the moment Birdie wished away the gingerbread people. And so the day began to warm, the snow melting away.

Claire and Max returned a few minutes later. Claire looked a bit confused. 'I went home to get something. But now I can't remember what it was,' she said. 'Why is everything so wet? Did it rain?'

'Just a drop!' Flick's dad replied. 'And how are you feeling, Mrs Mortlake?'

'A tad odd!' Mrs Mortlake said. She took a few sips of her iced tea. As she put her glass back down, she looked at the tin of shortbread Flick's dad had given her.

'Oh, wouldn't it be lovely to win that trip,' she said.

Flick began to understand what had happened. Birdie had wished for *all* the afternoon's wishes to be undone. And she'd made Mrs Mortlake and Claire forget about them. This meant Mrs Mortlake had no longer won the lovely trip to Scotland.

Flick felt terrible. Poor Mrs Mortlake. She'd been so excited about getting to visit her family. Flick thought about how much she was missing Granny Aggie. She knew what to do. She looked up at her parents, who nodded. They thought it was the right thing to do too.

Flick leaned towards Birdie and was about to whisper in her little sister's ear when a phone began to ring.

It was Mrs Mortlake's.

'Hello?' she answered. 'Yes, it is … I did?

Really? … Well, thank you very much! I'll be there.'

Mrs Mortlake hung up. She was grinning from ear to ear again. 'I won that trip to Scotland! Can you believe it?'

'We can!' Flick's mum and dad said.

'Gah?' Birdie said.

Flick was confused. Birdie must have made the wish without her hearing it. She stuck her head under the table.

'Imp,' she said. 'There is to be *no twisting* Mrs Mortlake's wish.' Mrs Mortlake was so excited to see her family. Flick was really happy for her. But how could she make absolutely sure the imp hadn't twisted the wish in some way?

It didn't take long to work out how. 'If you twist that wish, there will be none of Dad's special trifle for you on Christmas Day.'

The imp chewed on a musk stick thoughtfully. 'What's trifle?'

'Jelly. Custard. Sponge. Cream. Peaches. You would like it. A lot.'

'Ooohhh. I *do* like the sound of that. But the funny thing is, I can't twist that wish.'

Flick paused. 'You can't? Why not?'

'Because, this time, it wasn't a wish. Mrs Mortlake won the trip for real!'

12

One last wish

The afternoon tea wrapped up shortly after Mrs Mortlake's phone call. Mrs Mortlake needed to pack for her trip and Claire took Max for a nap. Oli bolted home to return Rosie's bed and costume. Then he came back to help Flick clear the table.

As Flick and Oli ferried bowls and cups into the house, Flick thought about the day. The ginger plants growing in the living room. The funny imp ornaments on Mrs Mortlake's Christmas tree. The winter wonderland in her back garden. And the naughty gingerbread people.

Flick laughed out loud as she remembered the gingerbread person with fangs shaking its fist at Mrs Mortlake.

There was only one thing she was sad about – that Granny Aggie hadn't been here to see it all. They would miss her so much this Christmastime.

Flick ducked under the table. Birdie was down there with the imp.

Flick took a deep breath. She might regret this, but she just couldn't help herself. It was Christmas. Granny Aggie had always said it was a magical time. Maybe this time the magic would go her way.

'You know,' she said to the imp. 'Mrs Mortlake's pretty busy packing. And then she has her flight tomorrow morning. I don't think she'll have much time to look into our back garden.'

The imp stopped nibbling its gingerbread for a moment. 'So?'

Flick leaned over and whispered to Birdie.

'Gah!' Birdie clapped her hands. **'Gah, gah, gah.'**

'Er, Flick?' Oli's voice came from above

the table. 'There seems to be a pool in your backyard.'

Flick grinned. 'I thought there might be. Come on, let's go see.'

Birdie crawled out from under the table. Flick picked her up and the three of them raced over to the back corner of the garden. There, a sparkling blue pool had magically appeared behind a glass fence.

Oli looked at Flick, who shrugged. 'It's just that it's almost Christmas. It's meant to be a really hot one this year. And with Mrs Mortlake gone …'

Oli peered doubtfully into the water. 'What do you think the twist will be? Are there sharks in the pool?'

As he said this, several items appeared on the surface of the water. They floated lazily past.

'Gah!' Birdie clapped her hands again.

There was the twist.

An inflatable snack float, complete with treats and mocktails. And another float that looked like a doughnut. Where the imp was now lounging.

Flick and Oli both burst out laughing.

As Flick laughed, she realised her heart felt much lighter than it had that morning. Granny Aggie might not be here in person, but she was here in another way. She'd shown Flick how *she* could make Christmas special for other people. For Mrs Mortlake. For Mr Tran. For the imp. For *everyone*.

Including herself.

The end

Read *The Party Wish*
to find out how
the magic began!

1

Birdie's favourite book

'And that was how Petunia the unicorn celebrated her super-fabulous first birthday.'

Flick closed the cover of the picture book she was holding. She'd read *Petunia the Unicorn's Super-fabulous First Birthday* hundreds of times now.

It felt like thousands.

Flick leaned forward and peered inside the cot.

Phew. It looked like her little sister, Birdie, was finally asleep.

Flick went to get up.

A small hand made its way through the railings. It tapped the book.

Again.

Flick sighed. 'Can't we read the donkey book, Birdie? Or the sheep book?' Those books were funny. Flick enjoyed reading them over and over again.

Tap tap.

Ugh. There were too many books about unicorns. *Petunia the Unicorn's Super-fabulous First Birthday* was the worst unicorn book of all. Flick was tired of Petunia's super-fabulous first birthday. She'd had enough of reading about the cake made of clouds. She'd had enough of reading about the rainbow slide made of sour straps. And she'd *definitely* had enough of reading about the ball pit filled with marshmallows.

'I wish we could have a Petunia party so you could see how silly it would be,' Flick said.

'Gah, gah, gah!' Birdie said.

'Okay. But only once more,' Flick said. If Birdie wanted the book again, she would read it over. It was very important to Flick to be the best big sister ever. She took

Petunia the Unicorn's
Super-fabulous First Birthday

a deep breath and opened the book to the first page.

'And that was how Petunia the unicorn celebrated her super-fabulous first birthday.' Flick finished up.

Again, she closed the book.

Again, she leaned forward.

Birdie's eyes were shut!

Slowly, quietly, Flick stood. Birdie made a noise and Flick froze. In the cot, Birdie smacked her lips. She smiled. But her eyes didn't open.

Flick grinned. It looked like Birdie was dreaming about eating cloud cake.

Flick had to admit – sometimes Birdie could be pretty cute.

Flick went into the kitchen and sat down at the bench. 'Birdie's asleep. I had to read the Petunia book. Twice.'

'Oh, dear.' Flick's mum looked up from the frypan she was washing.

'That was very nice of you,' Flick's dad said, tea towel in his hand.

'It's a very silly book,' Flick continued. 'A rainbow slide made out of sour straps would not be slippery, it would be rough. A marshmallow pit would be super sticky. A cake made of clouds would be wet.

And if unicorns were real, they would *not* poop cupcakes.'

'I believe you might be right about that,' Flick's dad said.

'Fingers crossed Birdie falls in love with a new book soon,' Flick's mum said.

'I hope so,' Flick replied. 'Because I have had enough of Petunia and her party.'

Add these magical books to your wish list!

Allison Rushby made a wish when she was six years old. She wished to be a ballerina with pierced ears. Not long after this, she wrote her very first book (not about a ballerina) and decided to be an author with pierced ears instead. She went on to write many more books, for both adults and children, though none of them were sticky-taped together like that first one. She lives in Brisbane with her family and her two not very useful assistants, Harry the Bordoodle and Titus the Sphynx. To learn more about Allison, visit www.allisonrushby.com.

When **Karen Blair** was young she wished she could see the fairies in the garden and would sometimes leave baked beans out for them. She also wished that she could draw all day and now the wish has come true! Karen loves to illustrate characters that are young, old and in between. She lives in Fremantle, Western Australia, with her husband, two children and a small dog called Dobby, who thinks he's a cat. To learn more about Karen, visit www.karenblair.com.au.

First published 2023 by University of Queensland Press
PO Box 6042, St Lucia, Queensland 4067 Australia

University of Queensland Press (UQP) acknowledges the Traditional Owners and their custodianship of the lands on which UQP operates. We pay our respects to their Ancestors and their descendants, who continue cultural and spiritual connections to Country. We recognise their valuable contributions to Australian and global society.

uqp.com.au
reception@uqp.com.au

Cover design by Mika Tabata
Cover and internal illustrations by Karen Blair
Author photograph by Little Family Photo Co.
Illustrator photograph by Jessica Wyld
Typeset in 14.75/24 pt Minion Pro by University of Queensland Press
Printed in Australia by McPherson's Printing Group

Australian Government | Australia Council for the Arts

University of Queensland Press is assisted by the Australian Government through the Australia Council, its arts funding and advisory body.

A catalogue record for this book is available from the National Library of Australia.

ISBN 978 0 7022 6636 2 (pbk)
ISBN 978 0 7022 6928 8 (epdf)
ISBN 978 0 7022 6929 5 (epub)

University of Queensland Press uses papers that are natural, renewable and recyclable products made from wood grown in well-managed forests and other controlled sources. The logging and manufacturing processes conform to the environmental regulations of the country of origin.

FSC www.fsc.org MIX Paper | Supporting responsible forestry FSC® C001695